**RICHTON PARK
PUBLIC LIBRARY DISTRICT**
4045 SAUK TRAIL
RICHTON PARK, ILLINOIS 60471

DEMCO

Rosita's Calico Cat

By Emily Thompson ◆ Illustrated by Tom Brannon

RICHTON PARK PUBLIC LIBRARY
RICHTON PARK, ILLINOIS

Featuring Jim Henson's Sesame Street Muppets™

A SESAME STREET/GOLDEN BOOK

Published by Western Publishing Company, Inc.,
in conjunction with Children's Television Workshop.

One day Elmo stopped by Hooper's Store for an ice cream soda and found his friend Rosita looking sad.

"Rosita, what is the matter?" he asked, sitting down beside her.

"Oh, Elmo," said Rosita. "I am so worried. My little **gata** is lost."

"Your what?" asked Elmo.

"My cat," said Rosita. "My sweet little calico **gata**. She did not come home last night, and I can't find her anywhere."

"Elmo will help you look for your **gata**," said Elmo. "Maybe Grover and his mommy have seen your **gata**."

"**Hola**," said Rosita.

Elmo looked at Rosita. "That word sounded almost like hello."

"**Hola** means hello," said Rosita. "I said hello to Grover and his **madre**, his mother."

"**Hola**, Rosita," said Grover's mother.

"Have you seen my **gata**?" asked Rosita. "She is lost."

"We will help you find her," said Grover and his **madre**.

First they looked in the park. They looked under benches and behind bushes without any luck, until . . .

"Rosita! Over here!" called Grover. "I, Grover the Helper, have found your **gata**!" He pointed to a brown tail sticking out from under a bush.

"That is a very big **gata**!" said Grover.

"That is not a kitty," said Rosita. "That is Snuffy's **hermana**."

"**Hermana**?" echoed Grover.

"Sister," said Rosita. "Snuffy's sister, Alice! **Hola**, Alice! **Hola**, Snuffy!"

"Oh, I am so embarrassed!" said Grover. "And I am so sorry, Alice!"

Just then Farley and his brother rode by.
"**Hola**, Rosita," said Farley. "**Hola**, everyone. This is
my little brother, Freddie."

"**Hola**, Farley. And **hola** to your **hermano**, Freddie,"
said Rosita. "Have you seen my little calico cat?"

"No," said Farley, "but we saw Natasha and her
father at the playground. We could ask them."

"**Hola**, Natasha!" called Rosita to the furry little monster on the baby swing. "You must be her **padre**," she said to Natasha's father.

"Yes, I am her **padre**," said her father.

"**Hola**," said Rosita, shaking hands. "Do you know
Elmo? And here are Grover and his **madre** and Snuffy
and his **hermana** and Farley and his **hermano**.
Everyone, this is Natasha's father—her **padre**."

"Hello, everybody!" said Natasha's father.

"Have you seen my **gata**—my cat?" asked Rosita.

"No, I am sorry," said Natasha's father.
"Come on, everybody," said Grover. "There is
Barkley the dog. Maybe he has seen your cat."

"Barkley! Here boy," yelled Grover.

"Good boy, Barkley," said Grover. "Say hello to Rosita."

"WOOF!" said Barkley.

"**Hola**, Barkley," said Rosita. "What a big **perro** you are! Have you seen my little **gata**?"

"WOOF! WOOF! WOOF!" Barkley yelped excitedly. He jumped up and ran toward Sesame Street.

"Follow that **perro**!" yelled Rosita.

Natasha and her **padre**, Farley and his **hermano**,
Snuffy and his **hermana**, Grover and his **madre**, Elmo,
and Rosita all ran as fast as they could after Barkley.

Finally Barkley came to a stop beside Oscar's trash
can. "WOOF! WOOF! WOOF!" he barked.

"Hey, what's all the racket?" yelled Oscar, popping
up out of his can.

"**Hola**, Oscar," said Rosita. "Have you seen my cat?"

"No," said Oscar with a scowl. "And I don't want any cute little cats roaming around here. Now scram!"

SLAM! went the lid of the trash can.

Barkley had stopped barking and was sniffing around behind Oscar's trash can.

"What is it, **perro**?" asked Elmo. And he followed Barkley behind the boxes and crates.

A few seconds later Elmo ran out again!
"Rosita! Come look!" he said, tugging on Rosita's
arm.

There, nestled in an empty crate, was Rosita's cat. Cuddled around her were six tiny newborn kittens.

"**Gatitos**!" cried Rosita. "One, two, three, four, five, six beautiful kittens!"

"Oooooh," said Natasha.

"Yucch!" said Oscar, popping up for a look.

"SLURP!" said Barkley, giving the new **madre** a big wet kiss.

"My cat has a **familia**!" said Rosita.

"That sounds like it means family," said Farley.

"That's exactly what it is," said Rosita. "An adorable new **familia**."

Here are all the new words that Rosita taught her friends:

cat
gato
(GAH-toe)
or
gata
(GAH-tah)

Hello
Hola
(OH-lah)

mother
madre
(MAH-dray)

sister
hermana
(air-MAH-nah)

brother
hermano
(air-MAH-no)

father
padre
(PAH-dray)

dog
perro
(PEHR-roh)

kittens
gatitos
(gah-TEE-toes)

family
familia
(fah-ME-lee-ah)